Harry Moves House

Chris Powling
and Scoular Anderson

Collins

Look out for more *Jets* from Collins

Jessy Runs Away • Best Friends • **Rachel Anderson**
Ivana the Inventor • Ernest the Heroic Lion Tamer • **Damon Burnard**
Two Hoots • Almost Goodbye Guzzler • **Helen Cresswell**
Shadows on the Barn • **Sara Garland**
Nora Bone • The Mystery of Lydia Dustbin's Diamonds • **Brough Girling**
Thing on Two Legs • Thing in a Box • **Diana Hendry**
Desperate for a Dog • More Dog Trouble • **Rose Impey**
Georgie and the Dragon • Georgie and the Planet Raider • **Julia Jarman**
Cowardy Cowardy Cutlass • Free With Every Pack • **Robin Kingsland**
Mossop's Last Chance • Mum's the Word • **Michael Morpurgo**
Hiccup Harry • Harry's Party • Harry the Superhero • Harry with Spots On
• **Chris Powling**
Rattle and Hum, Robot Detectives • **Frank Rodgers**
Our Toilet's Haunted • **John Talbot**
Rhyming Russell • Messages • **Pat Thomson**
Monty the Dog Who Wears Glasses • Monty's Ups and Downs • **Colin West**
Ging Gang Goolie, it's an Alien • Stone the Crows, it's a Vacuum Cleaner •
Bob Wilson

First published by A & C Black Ltd in 1993
Published by Collins in 1994
10 9 8 7
Collins is an imprint of HarperCollins*Publishers*Ltd,
77–85 Fulham Palace Road, Hammersmith, London W6 8JB

ISBN 0 00 674515-6

Text © 1993 Chris Powling
Illustrations © 1993 Scoular Anderson

The author and the illustrator assert the moral right to be identified as the author and the illustrator of the work.
A CIP record for this title is available from the British Library.

Printed in Great Britain by
Clays Ltd, St Ives plc

It was all my little sister's fault.

I mean, she wasn't even *born* yet
and already she was causing a fuss.

A fuss?

Sam and Thundercat weren't keen on moving any more than I was.

I also knew that Mum had made up her mind about moving so it was no use arguing. Especially as Dad seemed to agree with her.

'Cheer up, Harry,' he said. 'The
new house will be smashing,
I promise. And you can help us
choose it if you like.'

8

Funny? Who was being funny?

I was dead serious as it happened. What was the point of buying a new house if it looked just like the old one except a baby sister-size bigger?

The next few weeks were really awful
– really and *truly* awful.
We plodded round house . . .

. . . after house . . .

. . . after house.

Some were new, some were old.
Some were tall, some were broad.

Some were fusspot tidy,
some were so pigsty messy even
I wouldn't have lived there.
BUT ALL OF THEM WERE
BORING.

What I
wanted –

what I really, really wanted – was a
moated castle-with-lighthouse that
looked a bit haunted grange-like
apart from its swimming pool and
helicopter pad. We didn't see a
single one. Not one.

In the end, Mum and Dad settled
for a house that was exactly like our
old one except a baby sister-size
bigger. And a whole heap scruffier.

'That's assuming we can sell *our*
house,' Mum sighed. 'No one's even
come to look at it yet. If we don't
find a buyer soon we won't be able
to move after all.'

But I realised it now . . .

. . . and by the time the first people arrived on our doorstep, I was ready for them.

 MID-TERRACE TRADITIONAL VILLA
In quiet residential area

Containing:

LOUNGE: with bay window formation and log-effect living flame gas fire. Pleasing wall-covering. T.V. aerial and ample power sockets.

KITCHEN: Fully-fitted matching cupboards and work surfaces. Stainless steel sink with mixer tap. Two ceiling lights. Plumbing for washing machine. Italian-style tiled floor.

HALL: Stairway to upper floor. Spacious walk-in cupboard with shelf and six coat hooks.

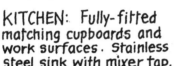
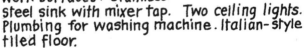

They had a piece of paper from the estate agent called the 'house details'.

This told them all about our
house . . . well, *nearly* all about
our house.

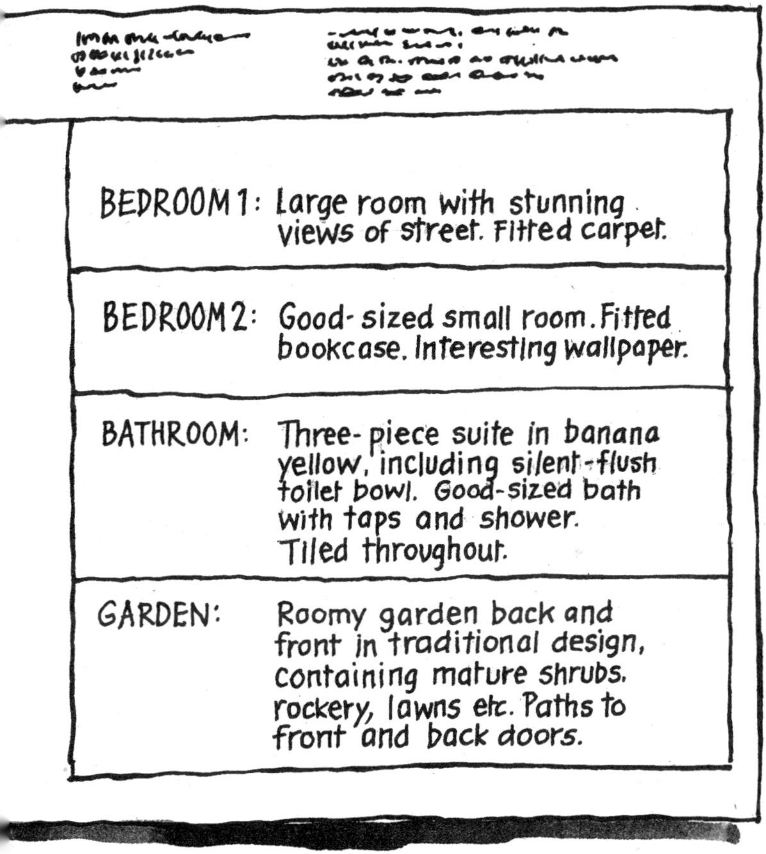

(handwritten scribble)	*(handwritten scribble)*

BEDROOM 1:	Large room with stunning views of street. Fitted carpet.
BEDROOM 2:	Good-sized small room. Fitted bookcase. Interesting wallpaper.
BATHROOM:	Three-piece suite in banana yellow, including silent-flush toilet bowl. Good-sized bath with taps and shower. Tiled throughout.
GARDEN:	Roomy garden back and front in traditional design, containing mature shrubs, rockery, lawns etc. Paths to front and back doors.

There were a few facts missing,
I reckoned, and I felt it was
my duty to pass them on.

About the damp patches, for instance.

About the plans to build a
motorway straight through the
house.

About our antique plumbing and
how much fun it could be.

About the low-flying aircraft
(only at night).

About the ghost.

About what interesting neighbours we had.

Most of what I said was a bit true,
though I did exaggerate a little,
I admit – just to make our house
sound *interesting*, you understand.

Eventually, I got so fed up with
being an estate agent, I decided to
give out 'house details' of my own
as a short cut.

32 Winchester Avenue

Hall: very dark and creepy at night. Stairs have seven squeaky floorboards.

LOUNGE: Really <u>boring</u> view. The wallpaper above the door keeps peeling off. Dad has stuck it back <u>hundreds</u> of times. The cat was sick on the carpet under the window.

Kitchen: The cat flap in the back door bangs when the wind blows. There's a gap beside the cooker full of things that have dropped down, like baked beans and bits of cabbage.

Bathroom: If you turn on
           the hot tap in the
           bath ∧ the water
             really hard
           scooshes out from
           under the third tile
           on the left. It takes
           about ten tries to
           flush the loo. (you
           really need the knack.)

Bedroom 1: Really boring, cold
           room. Really draughty
           all the year round.

Bedroom 2: Secret hidey-hole
           under the carpet behind
           the door - good for
           keeping things. Window
           slithers down and chops
           off your fingers if you're
           not careful.

Garden: Full of boring shrubs
           and things. Most of them
           are dead. Full of smelly
           old dog bones.

It was a big mistake. The very first time I handed them over, the couple-plus-soppy-kid laughed so much they offered to buy the house straight away. For once in my life I was speechless.

As for Mum and Dad . . . they didn't know whether to thank me or give me a clip round the ear.

After this everything went quiet for months and months. Nothing much happened except phone calls and meetings (yawn-yawn).

I almost forgot we were moving at all.

Except Mum was getting fatter and fatter.

And the couple-plus-soppy-kid kept paying visits to measure up and 'get the feel of their new home'. *Their* home?
The cheek of it! This was *my* home.

Even worse, Mum and Dad were so worried about the move they were practically wetting themselves about what might go wrong. 'Suppose there's another break in the chain?' Mum asked.

The chain? What's our loo got to do with it?

Not <u>that</u> chain. The chain of people buying houses, Mum means. If somebody drops out it delays all of us.

It sounded to me as if the whole world was moving house. Why was everyone so fidgety all of a sudden?

When the removal day finally arrived it was time to shift everything we owned – and I do mean *everything*. 'Wrap anything breakable in newspaper,' Mum said.

29

Luckily, she thought this was funny. She told me that when we got to the new house we'd put butter on Thundercat's paws.

I think she was trying to cheer me up.

But it just made me feel worse.
Minute by minute our house was
getting emptier and emptier. Soon
the couple-plus-soppy-kid would
take it over altogether.

The soppy kid?

That gave me an idea. At least
I could make sure *she* never forgot
moving day.

I left a special surprise for her on top of the door into my – I mean, *her* – room, where there was no chance at all she'd miss it.

While Mum and Dad said goodbye
to our old house, I sat in the van
with the driver and his mate.

I didn't even wave when the van turned the corner into the main road and our old house was gone forever.

We were soon at our new house.
Much *too* soon if you ask me.
Now it was empty it looked giant-
size – and giant-scruffy.

'Why don't we buy the van instead?'
I suggested. 'Then we could leave
all our stuff in it – and when we
fancy another move we can just
drive round the corner.'

Funny? I wasn't trying to be funny
– I was trying to be serious.

Moving in was serious, you can bet. Mum sat on a chair in the middle of the lounge and gave out instructions about where to put things.

Honestly, it was just as bad as moving *out*.

Hours and hours later, the removal
van drove off leaving us with piles
of furniture covered in dust-sheets
in every room.

Dad started on the decorating straight away.

And I really tried my hardest.

Was it my fault
I had problems
with the
paint rollers . . .

. . . and the paintpot?

And Dad's ladder
would probably
have fallen over,
even if I hadn't
leant on it to admire
my painting.

'Go and help Mum, Harry,' Dad snarled.

'She's lying down again listening to that baby *laughing*,' I said bitterly.

Keep me *amused*? What was amusing about this monster of a house?

I'd had enough of it already. As Dad
went on sloshing paint everywhere
it began to look more and more like
an indoor Arctic wilderness – except
without the penguins and polar
bears to make it interesting.
Instead, I had to make do with Sam
and Thundercat . . .

Still, there was no need for Dad to lose his temper.

I could tell I wasn't wanted.

That's when I decided Sam and Thundercat and I would find somewhere else to live, somewhere warm and friendly that we were used to – Dad's greenhouse at our old home, for instance. So far as I knew, the couple-plus-soppy-kid hadn't even looked inside it.

So I packed up some bits and bobs we might need. I told Dad we were off to seek our fortune, and I didn't know when we'd be back.

He probably thought I was being funny. But I wasn't.
Good job I could remember the way home.

But why was it that the closer and closer we got to our old house the sadder and sadder I felt? Even Thundercat and Sam didn't look too happy. We didn't brighten up even when we discovered that the couple-plus-soppy-kid hadn't moved in yet and the house was still ours in a way.

I still felt like a trespasser as I slipped the catch on the kitchen window and climbed inside.

The house was empty and echo-y.

Now I felt like a ghost-kid with a ghost-dog and a ghost-cat.

'Whoo-ooo-ooo!' came the answer followed by 'woof-woof-woof!' and 'miaow-miaow-miaow!' from Sam and Thundercat. They got an answer too. 'Maybe we'll feel better if we go up to my room,' I said.

That was my *biggest* mistake of the day.

I wasn't at all surprised at the next
disaster. The front door burst open.

The trouble was, once we'd started
they soon forgot about my niceness.

It was just like a video-replay of everything I'd been through already (twice).

I thought it would never end.

I also had to deal with the soppy kid who kept kissing and cuddling Sam and Thundercat.

Any minute, I thought she was going to start on me.

At last we stopped for a breather.

I shook my head. By this time, even with their furniture only half-unpacked, our old house was a different place altogether.

So now we didn't really live *anywhere*, Sam and Thundercat and me.

It was starting to get dark as we
trudged back through the
BORING streets.

'We've been away so long I don't expect Mum and Dad will recognise us,' I said. 'And I won't recognise them. We'll have to start by explaining to each other who we are.'

I banged hard on our new front door. The man who answered looked at me hard.

I couldn't believe it. It was like my worst nightmare come true!
'Is that Harry?' came a voice down the stairs.

Was somebody ill? Had there been
an accident? I flew up those stairs
faster than a penguin with a polar
bear after it.

'Hello, Harry,' said Mum from
the bed.
'Hello, Harry,' said the new baby.
Well . . . she nearly said it. Because
I'd been right all along about her
being a girl. 'What do you think of
her?' Mum asked.

What could I say? She seemed so small and sweet, even my genius-brain let me down, for once.

Good job you didn't have her before we moved, Mum. Because she wouldn't look nearly as good wrapped in newspaper.

Don't ask me why this was so funny. It was ages before Mum and Dad stopped laughing.